For Edward and Emma Bowen,
who know the island well.

Text copyright © Elisabeth Beresford 1998
Illustrations copyright © Gillian Hunt 1998

First published in Great Britain in 1998
by Macdonald Young Books
an imprint of Wayland Publishers Ltd
61 Western Road
Hove
East Sussex
BN3 1JD

Find Macdonald Young Books on the internet at http://www.myb.co.uk

The right of Elisabeth Beresford to be identified as the author of
this Work and the right of Gillian Hunt to be identified as the
illustrator of this Work has been asserted by them in accordance
with the Copyright, Designs and Patents Act 1988.

Designed and Typeset by Backup Creative Service, Dorset DT10 1DB
Printed and bound in Belgium by Proost International Book Production

British Library Cataloguing in Publication Data available

ISBN 0 7500 2405 4

ELISABETH BERESFORD

Island Treasure

Illustrated by Gillian Hunt

Chapter One

With a sinking heart, Jon watched the island getting closer and closer. He hadn't wanted to come and stay with his Aunt Tilda and cousin Matty. He'd wanted to go to Greece with his parents like he usually did. He'd got friends there, there was windsurfing and waterskiing, and the sea was warm and flat.

Here the sea was choppy and cold. The island looked bleak and empty, with just trees and a few small stone houses.

Jon knew he was going to hate it and probably his relations as well.

The boat edged in sideways. A gangplank rattled over the side and, suddenly, Jon recognized Aunt Tilda amongst a small group of people on the quayside. Standing next to her was a girl of about his own age. She looked really bad-tempered. Jon's heart sank even further.

Out of the corner of her mouth Matty hissed at her mother, "Is that him? That tall gangly thing? He looks really cross."

"Ssh. They've been having a bad time since his father lost his job. Just smile! Remember he's your cousin, eh?"

Matty always knew when her mother was nervous because she went back to the old island habit of saying 'eh' all the time.

They all shook hands and Aunt Tilda said, "You're tall like your dad, eh? Welcome to the island. Was the crossing rough? The car's over here…"

Jon couldn't believe the car. He'd never seen one that was so old and battered. It rattled and clanked over the cobbles and it was a relief when they stopped in a quiet street in front of a small stone house.

Jon started to brag over tea. He'd never been in such a small house before with such thick walls and low ceilings. He talked about how big his house was and about the tennis court and the two cars... He didn't mean to do it, but the words just came pouring out before he could stop them. At last Matty could hold her tongue no longer. How dare her gangly cousin make fun of her home and show off about his own!

"We can't have big houses and smart cars on the island," she said. "We have to work hard for our livings here, because there's only just enough jobs to go round…" Too late she remembered her mother telling her that Jon's father was out of work.

There was a terrible silence during which all three of them stared at the tablecloth. The rest of the meal was eaten in silence and Matty actually offered to do the washing up so that she could escape to the kitchen.

Chapter Two

Things were a little better in the morning, because the sun was shining and the sky was bright blue. Matty took a deep breath and had a go at making friends.

"It's nearly the low lows – that's the very low tides," she said to Jon. "It only happens twice a year. Would you like to come crabbing with me and my friends round the rocks?"

"Er," said Jon. The truth was, he was a bit nervous about the sea when it wasn't calm and warm. And he didn't like the idea of catching crabs with sharp claws. But he couldn't admit all that to Matty.

Luckily, help was at hand because Aunt Tilda said, "Oh, Matty, I thought you were going to help me with the Island Hall Jumble Sale, eh?"

Usually Jon would have run a mile from a jumble sale, but now he leapt at it.

"I'll give you a hand," he offered.

"That is kind," said Aunt Tilda, beaming at him. Matty went off on her battered old bike promising to come back with a crab tea. Jon was just getting into the rusty car when the front door opposite opened and a man with white hair and thick spectacles appeared clutching a heavy cardboard box.

"Caught you," he said, beaming. "I've got some jumble for you."

"Jon, this is Mr Gatrell," said Aunt Tilda. "He's in charge of the museum."

"Welcome to the island," said Mr Gatrell. "You'll probably be down on the beach most of the time, but do look into the museum if you've got time. We've got some exciting stuff, including a few things from the Occupation."

Jon looked at him blankly. Mr Gatrell smiled, patted him on the back and strode off. Aunt Tilda laughed and above the roar and rattle of the car she explained.

"The Occupation was when your grandad was a boy. There were enemy soldiers on the island, thousands of them. They built fortresses and there were guns and barbed wire everywhere. Most of the islanders escaped, but some were left behind. By the end of the war, they had

disappeared...

"When it was all over, some families came back. They said people must have starved because there wasn't a limpet on the rocks or a bird in the fields. They'd all been eaten. But that's enough of that. What's Mr Gatrell given us?"

It was a box of dusty old books and comics. Jon liked books and he helped sort out the bookstall in the Island Hall. As a reward he was told he could take a book for himself. He was tossing up between one on space travel and an adventure story when a familiar voice said, "Hi".

It was Matty. She shifted from foot to foot and then said in a gruff voice, "I'm sorry about what I said about people not having jobs…"

Jon stared at the pile of books in front of him.

"Doesn't matter. Dad'll get another job quite soon. And I shouldn't have said that about your house. I expect you need thick walls in the winter…"

"I'll give you a hand if you like," Matty said. She picked up one of the dusty books. As she did so, a very small notebook slid out from inside the cover.

Jon picked up the tiny red notebook and glanced inside. Every small page was crammed with minute pencilled writing. He screwed up his eyes and read…

No tea. Gunfire in the night. Tuesday. Out early. Got under wire. Found two eggs. Ma pleased. Ran messages for THEM. Paid me three slices bread. Low lows soon. Crabs?

It was as though all the noise and bustle of the Island Hall had faded away and he was in another world. Inside the cover was written, "DANNY – 1944".

"What have you got there? You look all funny…"

Jon came back to the present with a thump. He hesitated about showing Matty his find. But if she hadn't moved the dusty book in the first place he might never have found it. He really wanted to share this strange secret with someone. Matty seemed about the only person who might understand… They went down to the beach.

She listened to him in silence and then smiled at him like a friend for the first time.

"That's clever, eh, you finding it..."

"We both did. Only we'll keep it a secret!"

"Our secret!"

Chapter Three

Not all of it was easy to read or understand. And the writing was so cramped and faded that they took it in turns to read. Danny's life was tougher than they could ever imagine, but he never complained, and sometimes he even made jokes. "Ma says my insides rumble like gunfire!" he wrote. Whenever he or his uncle trapped a rabbit, they had stew, but sometimes he and his family had to eat grass soup or limpets.

But the most sinister parts of the diary were the parts which told what THEY did.

THEY told the islanders to be inside their homes with the curtains drawn as soon as it was dark. THEY shelled and sank a ship from which there were no survivors. THEY forced Danny and other boys as young as fourteen to build huge fortresses.

THEY were the enemy soldiers…

26

Matty shivered as they read. It was all so different from the island she had known all her life. And then on the last page Jon made out the words, "Low lows. Wolf Rock. Found ship's treasure. Going back with spade. TREASURE!!!"

And there it ended. Jon and Matty looked at each other.

"Treasure!" said Matty. "Ma could have a washing machine and we could paint the house. Pink!"

"And I could help my dad," Jon said, "until... until he gets another job!"

Matty sighed. "Sorry, it's not mine. You found it."

"We can share. We found it together," Jon said.

They both stared at the sparkling sea which was ebbing away from them, and then Jon said, "Of course, we haven't actually found the treasure yet. I wonder what it is. Gold? Diamonds? It must have been on that ship that was sunk. But where do we look?"

"Wolf Rock," Matty said slowly. "Everyone's heard of it. It's right by the old wreck... but I've never seen it because it's under the sea..."

Jon's face fell. For one incredible moment it really had seemed as if all his family troubles were over, but now the treasure was vanishing again before they'd even found it.

"...under the sea," Matty went on, "except at the low lows. That's when the tide goes out a lot more than usual. It only happens twice a year and one of those times is right now!"

Even as she spoke, the sea was rippling further away from them and the grey slippery tops of more rocks were appearing. Jon forgot how nervous he'd felt about this great ocean with its huge breakers. He kicked off his shoes and rolled up his jeans.

"I'm not supposed to go too far out," Matty said nervously. "You see, once the tide turns it comes in really fast. As fast as you can run…"

But Jon wasn't going to be put off. It was now or never. He looked round at the beach. In the distance, a familiar figure was poking at the sand with a long stick.

"There's Mr Gatrell! He'll keep an eye on us," Jon said, shouting and waving. Mr Gatrell came over to join them.

"We're going after treasure," Jon said, "if you could sort of keep an eye on the tide and make sure we don't get cut off."

"Pleasure," said Mr Gatrell, sitting down on the nearest rock. "What sort of treasure may I ask?"

"Real, proper treasure," Jon said. "Come on, Matty. Let's find Wolf Rock!"

The sand was soft and warm and quite often something which was very much alive moved under Jon's feet, but he didn't care. He was determined to find the treasure. It was as if Danny had wanted to lead them to it.

Matty, who knew how strong the sea could be, and how fast the tide could turn, had one eye on the gentle waves and one eye on the shore. Mr Gatrell began to seem a long, long way away... And then straight ahead of them a sharp, three-cornered shape began to rise out of the waves.

"The wreck," Matty croaked. "That's the bow! Wolf Rock must be just about... oh!"

Just short of the wreck a new shape was coming into view. As the sea sank away from it they could see its sharp outline like the dripping open jaws of a great stone wolf.

Without a word, Jon and Matty splashed towards it. Dimly they could hear Mr Gatrell shouting.

"You'd better come back now. The tide'll turn any minute…" The sea sucked away from the rock and as it did so Jon saw the square shape of a chest. It was covered in slimy weeds, but he knew this was it… Danny's Treasure!

The sea went calm for a moment and then a small ripple came towards them. The tide was starting to turn.

"Quick!" Jon shouted. There was a slimy handle at one end. He wrapped both hands round it and pulled with all his strength as Matty pushed. For a moment nothing happened and then slowly, reluctantly, the chest lurched out of its ancient hiding place.

"We must hurry," Matty said
breathlessly.

Jon couldn't speak. He was too excited.
It didn't matter that they were both
soaking wet and that the sea was starting
to race towards them.

Jon gripped the handle tightly and
began to heave the chest to where Mr
Gatrell was now shouting at them.

"Come on, the tide's turned. Come
on!"

Chapter Four

Aunt Tilda wasn't too pleased to have
three dripping wet bodies in her scrubbed
kitchen, let alone a filthy old chest which
was starting to smell horrible.

Jon, Matty and Mr Gatrell all began to talk at once. Matty got the crowbar out of the garden shed and Jon and Mr Gatrell somehow managed to force open the lid of the chest. Seaweed and muck went in all directions. Everybody crowded round and then hastily stepped back as an awful smell rose out of the chest.

Bravely Jon put his hand into it and scooped out a handful of smelly mud and tangled seaweed. Then he found an old tin. He ran some water over it, sniffed and Matty silently handed him a tin opener.

Jon felt his heart sinking and sinking as his hopes began to disappear. There was a long silence and then Mr Gatrell said, "I think it's what we used to call bully beef. That's what all these tins were filled with – tinned meat. Only most of it's rotted away.

This seems to be the only undamaged tin – that's why the bully beef's stayed fresh after all these years."

Jon felt as if he'd stepped into black space. It was all over, his wonderful dream of treasure and helping his father. And there went Aunt Tilda's washing machine and Matty's dream of a bright pink house… Dimly he heard Mr Gatrell say, "To a boy who was starving this would have been the best treasure in the world. You couldn't eat gold or diamonds…"

Jon nodded. He couldn't speak. He hardly listened to what the others were saying until Mr Gatrell said, "Could I perhaps see Danny's diary?"

Silently, Jon handed the small red notebook to him.

Mr Gatrell sat down at the kitchen table and slowly turned the tiny pages with their faded cramped writing. Then he said very quietly, "But this is truly amazing. It's a boy's record of what happened here on the island during the Occupation. No records were ever kept and it's always been a mystery as to what went on. How people survived and what happened to them. Now it's all here in this tiny diary…"

Jon and Matty stared at him. In a rather shaky voice Mr Gatrell went on, "This is your treasure, Jon. Danny's diary. It's a true Island Treasure and it could become very, very famous and worth a great deal. People all over the world will want to read about it. It's unique. It's wonderful! And you rescued it!"

Nobody spoke for a moment and then Mr Gatrell shook Jon's hand. Aunt Tilda threw her arms round him and kissed him on both cheeks. Matty grinned from ear to ear.

At last Jon managed to speak.

"It was both of us. It was Matty and me that found it. No, it was the three of us – Danny as well. Thanks, Danny! That's good – eh?"

Look out for more titles in the Red Storybooks series:

Lizzy's War by Elisabeth Beresford
The first book about Lizzy's wartime adventures with Miss Damps.

Lizzy Fights On by Elisabeth Beresford
In this second story about Lizzie, news comes that her father
might be in a prison camp. As Lizzy helps Miss Damps with the
war effort – collecting scrap metal, saving clothing coupons –
she tries to remember the father who left so long ago...

Thomas and the Tinners by Jill Paton Walsh
Thomas works in the tin mine where he meets some fairy miners
who cause him a great deal of trouble – but then bring him good
fortune. WINNER OF THE SMARTIES PRIZE.

Princess by Mistake by Penelope Lively
Would you believe it if your sister were suddenly kidnapped by a
knight in full armour riding an enormous black horse? And what
would you if you were then armed with a sword, a packet of
gobstoppers and a comic and told to rescue her?

The Tall Story by Frieda Hughes
Micky is always telling lies. Great big whopping ones. But when he
goes to stay with his grandmother by the sea, strange things start
to happen. Everything he lies about comes true...

You can buy all these books from your local bookseller, or they can
be ordered direct from the publisher. For more information about
Storybooks, write to: *The Sales Department, Macdonald Young Books,
61 Western Road, Hove, East Sussex BN3 1JD*